SCAR AND THE WOLF

BY JEFF WILLIAMS

ILLUSTRATED BY
MADELINE BARBER

"Scar and the Wolf"
Text and illustrations copyright
©2022 by 320 Sycamore Studios.

All rights reserved.

No part of this book may be used or reproduced in any manner except for brief quotations intended for review.

For information, visit 320sycamorestudios.com.

ISBN: 978-1-7375589-0-3

First edition.

Design by Jennifer Playford at playfordstudios.com

320 Sycamore Studios
www.320sycamorestudios.com

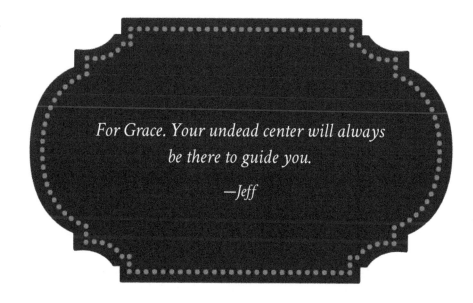

For Grace. Your undead center will always be there to guide you.

—*Jeff*

CONTENTS

	Introduction	1
1	Happy Unearthday, Scarlet	3
2	Rot Mitzvah	13
3	The Hideous Cloak	20
4	Forewarned is Forearmed	26
5	Zombies Roam the Street	32
6	A Friend Who Looks Like an Enemy	37
7	An Enemy Who Looks Like a Friend	48
8	Time to Do the Right Thing	56
9	Night Descends on Scarlet	63
10	All the Adventure Scarlet Can Stomach	70
11	What Goes Down Must Come Up	74
12	Totally Grossome	78
13	What Do You Wish For When You Have Everything?	82
14	The Best Things are Ings	90
	Afterword: And May Your Morning Bring Rebirth	96

Introduction

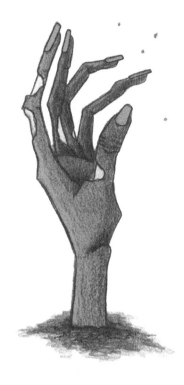

The world is dark and quiet, waiting for something to be born. Something not quite human, but not quite dead. A low mist crawls along the alleys of the town. A crow screeches down the dawn. Weak light seeps slowly into a cellar, where a patch of soil lies before a granite stone. Grass and mushrooms grow in tufts and clusters. The moist dirt is clotted, clumped, and freshly dug.

A blade of grass twitches, stills. It shivers again. Worms pause. Beetles wait. Suddenly, the grass across the dirt plot commences dancing. A small mound swells and falls. The world holds its breath. It waits. It waits. It waits…

Soil sprays upward. First dirt, then pebbles, then clods shower up and out as a fist punches from below into the rank air of morning. The fist flexes. It extends its fingers. Another fist bursts to the surface followed by forearms, elbows, shoulders, torso, and a face—an undead face moaning, "Brains…Brains!…BRAINS!"

Scarlet Bone blinked slowly awake.

"I love that dream," she croaked.

Chapter One
Happy Unearthday, Scarlet

Who are you, really, when you turn 13?

Yesterday you were a kid. Today you're stumbling into adulthood.

Part of you is ready to speak like an adult and think like an adult. Part of you wants Mom to make you breakfast.

Part of you is giddy with freedom. Part of you is terrified of freedom.

Part of you wants to talk about grownup things, like how much houses cost, and will they cost more next year?

And, part of you wants to daydream about that cape you saw at the market, how it shimmered like water, how beautiful you'd look in it.

Daydreams and responsibilities.

Work and play.

Have-to and want-to.

Turning 13 is an uncertain, lurchy place to be.

Yet somehow, every grownup zombie in Plainfield had managed it. It wasn't always graceful, since it's hard for zombies to be graceful in the best of times. And yes, some seemed like they never fully grew up while others seemed to grow up suspiciously fast.

Of course, sometimes a part—like an arm or a foot, say—wanted its independence so fiercely it fled its body.

But one way or another, all the conflicting parts eventually managed to move in the same direction.

I mean, these were zombies, after all.

Scarlet licked her lips, trying to imagine the brains from her dream into existence.

When that didn't work, she tried to fall back into the dream.

No luck.

She resigned herself to waking up.

When I get older, I can have brains whenever I want, she thought. *Wait. I AM older.*

She rose from her bedbox—spraying dirt across her bedroom floor—and lurched to her vanity table. She pulled down the face mask that kept her from inhaling clods and dust while she slept and leaned over to inspect her face in the mirror, her disappointment rising. Same hollow cheeks. Same dark circles under the eyes. Same matted brown hair. Same brown teeth. Same spongy nosehole.

Scarlet smacked her thighs with balled fists. "GARRR! I don't look a day older." Two dirt clods and three worms fell to the floor.

The worms wriggled back to the sanctuary of the dirtbox. (Worms are smarter than they're usually given credit for. Except when it rains.)

Scarlet shambled back to the edge of her bedbox, sat down, and had a think. Which was this: Maybe this day was going to be just another ordinary day. Maybe she was wrong to get her hopes up about it. Maybe she should go back to bed.

She dislodged a crusty booger from her nosehole and flicked it into her bed. Worm food.

She was lost in thought when the door at the top of the stairs banged open and her parents clattered down.

"*Happy unearthday to youuuu,*" sang her mother, Daisy.

"*Nyunnh nyunnh nyunnh nyunnh nyunnh nyunnh!*" warbled her father, Dr. Sigmund.

"Honey, your jaw!" whispered Daisy. Dr. Sigmund nodded and reached into the jaw-holster inside his tweed jacket. He pulled out the brass jawbone and snapped it into place. *Click-CLACK.*

"*Happy unearthday, dear Scar-let,*" they sang together.

"*Happy unearthday to y—*"

Daisy and Dr. Sigmund stopped at the bottom of the stairs when they saw their daughter.

"Darling, what's wrong?" asked Daisy. "It's your unearthday!"

"Nothing," muttered Scarlet.

"Nothing nothing or something nothing?" asked Dr. Sigmund. "Tell me, how do you feel?"

"Honey, not now," said Daisy. "She needs you to be her dad, not her therapist."

"It's okay, Mom," said Scarlet. "Something nothing. It's just…I guess I thought I'd wake up and feel…I don't know. Grown-up."

Daisy and Dr. Sigmund sidled to the bed and sat down next to Scarlet. Daisy's eyes darted briefly to the dirt trail on the floor. She almost said something to Scarlet about tidiness, then thought the better of it. Instead, she took Scarlet's hand in hers.

"It doesn't happen just like that," said Daisy. "Give it some time."

"Besides," said Dr. Sigmund. "By the end of the day, you may feel more grown-up than you want to."

"What do you mean?" asked Scarlet.

"Come upstairs," said Daisy. "We'll explain over breakfast."

"I made brainwaffles," said Dr. Sigmund, his eyes twinkling. "The House of Bone unearthday special."

Daisy patted Scarlet's hand. Dr. Sigmund kissed the top of her head. The three of them rose and shuffled toward the stairs.

"Where are you going, Sweetie?" asked Daisy.

"Uh, brainwaffles…?" said Scarlet.

"After your chores," cooed Daisy.

"You know the rules," said Dr. Sigmund. To emphasize his point, he strode to his daughter's bookshelf and pulled out a copy of *The Zombie Rules: How to Act in Every Situation,* by Hubris R. Rottenstuff. (It was one of three copies in the house.) "And if you forget, ask Hubris."

Scarlet groaned. "Seriously?"

"Absolutely," said Daisy. "Brush your skin. Rake the bed. Feed your fish. You know the drill."

Scarlet glanced at Chucky the Moldfish, inscrutable in his murky tank. She rolled her eyes. "Even on my unearthday."

"Even more so," said Daisy. She and Dr. Sigmund started up the stairs.

"The road to adulthood," sang Dr. Sigmund, "is paved with chores."

"Now hurry-hurry," Daisy insisted. "The clock is ticking. And," she couldn't resist the urge any longer, "don't forget to clean your floor."

Daisy and Dr. Sigmund clomped upstairs.

Why do I have to hurry-hurry? Scarlet wondered.

She flipped open the Rottenstuff book to the chapter on morning rules, though she didn't need to look to know it started with skin-brushing:

"Brush early and fast
to make your skin last.
Sweep dirt into bed,
to help clear your head."

Scarlet grabbed the first of her three skin-brushes—the steel-wool scrubber brush—from the vanity table drawer. She began to scour her arms, a process that invigorated all the molecules and microbes that mingled in her undead skin.

Zombie skin is a wicked tricky thing. Unless it is fastidiously tended, it sags. Or worse, it drops off in gloops and swatches, revealing all manner of squishy bits beneath.

So, zombies—well, all the best zombies—spent a lot of time caring for their unearthday suits, a process that involved skin-brushing, post-meal beetle cleanings, heat-drying when soggy, and quickly spackling fissures.

It was a lot of work. But it was pretty obvious when a zombie had stopped caring and let themself go. That wasn't going to be Scarlet. She cared rather a lot about her skin—and about her appearance in general. Almost to the extent that it didn't matter what kind of zombie she was like underneath. Almost.

Scarlet eyed her skin and gave a satisfied nod. Still, she was in a cranky mood. "What did they mean," she asked Chucky, "when they said that after today, I'd feel more grown-up?"

"Blurp-blurp," was all Chucky said.

Scarlet hoped it meant a shopping trip to the Plainfield Sanitary Market. "No, not just the market—Elysian," she explained to Chucky.

Scarlet replaced the scrubber skinbrush and took out the soother skinbrush, the one with horsehair bristles. As she swept it across her skin, puffs of dirt particles drifted to the mat below.

The jewel of the Plainfield fashion world was the Plainfield Market's Elysian clothing stall, and the jewel of Elysian was a cape that shimmered like water in the moonlight.

The dreams cape.

Scarlet wanted the dreams cape more than she had ever wanted anything. If she had the dreams cape, no one would ever look at her the same way again, especially not Jeminy Stinkpit. The sarcasm would end. The teasing would stop.

"Maybe we could even be friends, Chucky," said Scarlet.

"Blurp."

And if Jeminy accepted her, it would create a ripple effect across the school. If Jeminy accepted her, so too would the other members of the Plainfield Fashion Club for Girls—the Threadheads.

And if she didn't get the dreams cape?

Scarlet shuddered. It was too horrible to think about.

She lifted her right foot and swept it clean. She repeated the motion with her left foot.

Finally, she took out the third and last skin-brush, the shiner brush, and buffed gentle circles into her arms and legs to soften her skin.

Scarlet lifted the bedmat and dumped the dirt back into her bedbox. With the floor clean, Scarlet slipped into her favorite day dress—a light blue frock with sequins arranged in spiderweb patterns.

Scarlet dug her scoop into Chucky's scum bucket and slopped some breakfast into his tank. She was at the bottom of the stairs when she remembered one last chore: Rake the bed.

She groaned—*oh to be a grownup and free of these tiresome chores!*—but she was too wrapped in her dreams-cape daydream to feel annoyed. She opened the bottom drawer of the bedbox, pulled out the rake, and smoothed the dirt. Sort of. Actually, she left it lumpy and clumpy, not level like The Rules suggested. "Good enough," she shrugged, tossing the bedrake back in the drawer.

"Waffles!" called Daisy from upstairs.

"Coming!" Scarlet hollered, finally feeling some optimism about this whole growing-up idea.

Chapter Two
Rot Mitzvah

If Scarlet had to name her favorite smell, she would have a hard time choosing. Rotten eggs… swamp gas…sweat…morning breath…toe jam… animal droppings of all kinds…

How to pick just one?

But eventually, she would have said that the finest smell of all was the aroma of brainwaffles cooking in a waffle iron.

It should be noted that like all zombies, the zombies of Plainfield ate brains. They ate a lot of other foods, too, but they loved brains above all else. They had an infinite number of ways to prepare them and would eat them every chance they got. And if you're concerned about where the brains came from, don't be. Plainfield's zombies ate only brains from animals that had lived long happy lives and then died in their sleep of natural causes. Which, when you think about it, is rather civilized.

Scarlet's pale-green face lit up as she entered the kitchen. She sat down, tore open an envelope with her name on it, and began to read the unearthday card inside.

She opened her mouth. Closed it. Frowned. Read bits out loud.

"No presents 'til tonight…If I successfully complete a mission…buy my first haggis…woods…grandma…party…Threadheads…"

Dr. Sigmund set a plate of steaming brain-waffles in front of her.

She jabbed a finger at the card. "What does a real rot mitzvah mean? It just sounds like another big chore."

"Think of it as a project," said Dr. Sigmund.

"Project Haggis," Daisy cooed. "You know that 13th unearthdays are rot mitzvah days involving special tasks."

"Yeah," Scarlet fumed, "but Jeminy's task was to go to the market and shop."

"Which explains so much," said Dr. Sigmund under his breath.

Scarlet didn't notice the side-eye Daisy gave him. "And all Sparkle and Spangle had to do was pick what kind of brains they wanted in their unearthday cakes."

"Call us old-school," said Dr. Sigmund, "but we believe in a proper rot mitzvah."

The rot mitzvah was originally intended to signify a young zombie's transition into adulthood, and involved a test of spirit and resilience that left them with a feeling of honest accomplishment when it was done. As part of the ceremony, the teenager was asked to wear a special item of clothing—say an old stovepipe hat or a worn pair of hobnail boots or, in Scarlet's case, a cloak. The newly grownup zombie would then keep the clothing until it was time to pass it on to their own child.

At least, this was the rot mitzvah tradition until an unfortunate incident involving the youngest Judkins boy. While all of his parts had been recovered—eventually—grownups had in recent years been going easy on their children, and turning 13 wasn't the ordeal it used to be.

The Bones, however, respected tradition, and they wanted their daughter to have a proper coming-of-age.

"After all," said Dr. Bone, "the Judkins boy is fine now."

"Plus, you love haggis," said Daisy.

True. What zombie didn't love chopped-up hearts and lungs and livers and tongues stuffed into an animal stomach and boiled for hours? It paired especially well with unearthday braincake.

But that didn't mean Scarlet wanted to wait in line at the market and schlep a haggis through the woods to Grandma's house. "It's my unearthday," she said. "Isn't the food *your* job?"

Scarlet's brainwaffles were going cold. She halfheartedly slathered the stack in bugbutter and pond-scum syrup.

Daisy shook her head. "Not today."

"Trust us," said Dr. Sigmund.

Scarlet stabbed her fork into a hunk of brainwaffle and took a bite. She and her parents ate in silence for a few minutes.

Finally, Scarlet asked, "Who's going to be at the party?"

"All your classmates," said Daisy.

"Plus some of our friends," said Dr. Sigmund.

"The Threadheads," said Daisy.

"Jeminy," muttered Scarlet.

"She'll be there because she's a Threadhead…"

"…and because her mom's your boss," said Scarlet, glaring at her mother.

"…and Threadheads support each other," said Daisy, firmly.

Scarlet lowered her eyes.

Dr. Sigmund swallowed, set down his fork and patted Scarlet's wrist. She pulled her arm away. "Get to Grandma's at five o'clock," he said.

"We'll meet you there shortly after. The party starts at six. And Scarlet," he smiled, "it's going to be great."

"For you two. I'm doing all the work." Scarlet took a bite. "Why do I have to go through the woods by myself?"

"Your father has patients to see today," said Daisy, "and I have an open house. Don't worry, we'll give you money for the haggis."

"Plus a bit extra," said Dr. Sigmund, "so you can get yourself a treat."

Scarlet brightened. "Oh! How much extra?"

"What do you think, Daisy? Four bones?"

"I think five, Sig. It is a special day. How does that sound, Scarlet?"

The cape cost more. A LOT more.

Scarlet pointed her index finger at her mouth and made a retching sound.

"Scarlet, the world doesn't revolve around you just because you have an unearthday."

"Well, it should!"

Dr. Sigmund leaned back in his chair. "Scarlet, if you meet the day with the right frame of mind—like a grownup—you'll be amazed at the rewards."

Scarlet wanted to be treated like a grownup more than anything. But she wasn't about to admit that her father was right.

"That helps. Not." Scarlet pushed away from the table and clomped out of the kitchen.

Daisy called out one last instruction. "Don't forget to wear your red cloak!"

CHAPTER THREE
THE HIDEOUS CLOAK

Clothing traditions are weird. Why do we wear Christmas sweaters? Or wedding dresses? Or business suits? Or 13th unearthday cloaks?

If you ponder on it a while, though, there's usually some reason we do the things we do. Once you hold up an idea and look at it from a few different angles, you can still say, "No thank you. I will NOT wear that Christmas sweater." Or you can say, "I like how serious I feel in this business suit." Or, "I'll wear a wedding dress, but I'll do it MY way." But it's those multiple ways of looking at something that make a grownup a grownup. Which Scarlet wasn't. Yet.

Scarlet kept her best capes, cloaks, and dresses in the front of her closet. But because her mom had commanded it, she was now looking for one of her *worst* pieces of clothing. She reached back-back-back, past her out-of-fashion dresses, too-small trousers, and a pair of like-new overalls she'd never worn and always hated.

There at the back was the cloak. That hideous crimson cloak.

Scarlet grimaced as she tugged it from the closet.

To say it was a hand-me-down would be an insult to hand-me-downs. THIS cloak had been torn, stained, ripped, stitched, mended, cleaned, sewn, and lacquered over with weather sealant for so many generations that no one could remember when it was first made or what it had originally looked like.

Scarlet looked at Chucky Moldfish, doing slow laps in his tank.

Chucky Moldfish looked at Scarlet.

"Why, Chucky? Why do I have to wear this... this *tarp*?"

"Blurp."

Scarlet tossed the cloak onto her dirtbox and made ready to meet the morning.

Out of habit, she looked at the "body maintenance" instruction list tacked to the vanity mirror. Scarlet glowered at it, though inside she was glowering at her mom, her dad, the universe, anything that wasn't giving her what she wanted today.

She opened the tin of mouth moss, scrubbed a tuft across her teeth, then chewed it into a soft ball of cud. She worked it into a sodden lump, leaned her head back, and *Ptooey*! The cudball flew across the room and landed with a *splish* in Chucky's tank.

Scarlet tried to not think about the cloak. But, as typically happens when we try not to think about something, it was all she could think about.

Before the cloak was Scarlet's, it belonged to Daisy. Before that, to Scarlet's Grandma Bone. Before that, it had belonged to a long line of grandmas receding into the distant past.

Twice Scarlet had snuck the cloak into the donation box for CROAK—the City Refuge for Orphaned and Abandoned Kids. Daisy had found the cloak both times and warned Scarlet that a third would mean her removal from the Threadheads.

Scarlet dragged a comb through tangled mats of hair, then sprayed it with Mister Spritzer Rain Resister.

"On her 13th unearthday, every woman in the Bone family wears the cloak," Daisy had told her many times. "You keep it until you become a grownup and then you give it to the next girl in line."

"I'm not wearing it," Scarlet said to Chucky. "Time for a new tradition."

She pulled a snaker swab out of a jar and dabbed it in nose balm.

"If I ever have a daughter, she's getting the dreams cape."

Scarlet swirled the swab around her nosehole lining. She plunged it in and when she pulled it out, it was covered in black grime.

"And we can use the cloak for a doormat or a dog bed or something."

Scarlet looked in the mirror and nodded once. She was ready. She returned to the closet. "I'm a grownup now, and I can wear what I want." At the front hung her favorite item of clothing (at least until she got the dreams cape): a thin, white satin jacket she'd appliquéd with black and red corpse flowers. The Threadheads had almost been impressed.

She pulled her warthog-leather shoulder bag (made from the hide of a warthog that had died peacefully in its sleep of natural causes) off its closet peg and started upstairs.

"See ya later, Chucky," she called to the moldfish. She watched Chucky's dorsal fin cut the water like a shark's before he disappeared in tank-murk. Scarlet paused. *Like a shark.*

The shark thought made Scarlet think of Grandma Bone's famous trip-to-the-beach story. How she'd risked soggy skin to try swimming. How she'd ignored the shark warnings. How one shark thought her legs looked especially delicious. How—*chomp!*—there went her legs. Then Grandpa showed up (before he was Grandpa), wrapped Grandma in her cloak, and carried her like a sack of potatoes to the nearest Pick-A-Part body-part store to buy her a new pair of legs.

Grandma loved that cloak. Scarlet loved her Grandma.

"Argh!" she muttered. "I can't believe I'm doing this, Chucky." Scarlet retrieved the cloak and stuffed it in her bag.

"Hurry, Scarlet," her father called down to her. "The best haggi will be gone!"

Scarlet lurched upstairs.

Chapter Four
Forewarned is Forearmed

There are lots of terrible places to be in the world. Stuck at the bottom of a well. Mired in a leech-infested bog. Trapped in the back seat on a long, bumpy cart ride with nothing to read. Geometry class.

But the worst place to be stuck is in between. That place where you've outgrown the familiar.

You need to step into a new space, a bigger space, but you're not sure how to act when you get there.

The thing about growing up, though, is that if you're doing it right, you're *always* moving into a bigger, more uncomfortable space.

The secret is that you get comfortable with being uncomfortable.

I know. It sounds weird.

Anyway, that's where Scarlet was. She didn't want to hang around the house, but she was nervous about Project Haggis.

"What are the three rules of traveling?" asked Dr. Sigmund.

Scarlet shifted her weight from one sequined sneaker to the other and stared up at the entry ceiling. "One. Be on time," she yawned.

Daisy plucked a bit of fluff off Scarlet's jacket.

"Yes. Get to Grandma's by five. Party at six," said Dr. Sigmund.

"You already told me," said Scarlet.

"Rule number two?" asked Dr. Sigmund.

"Stay on the path."

Daisy tucked Scarlet's hair behind her ears.

"Indeed. You'll be fine in the woods. When you're in the market, the stay-on-the-path rule means stay away from the back stalls. Last rule?"

"Don't talk to strangers."

Daisy licked her thumb and rubbed a tiny brain-waffle crumb off Scarlet's cheek.

"Close."

"Huh?" Scarlet thought a moment. "Oh, right, don't talk to *strange* strangers."

"Bingo," said Dr. Sigmund. "The back stalls are full of them."

Daisy stood back and regarded Scarlet. "You really do look grown-up," she said.

"When you get to the market," Dr. Sigmund continued, "get in the haggis line right away. Right away. Because it's probably going to be long and you want to give yourself time to get to Grandma's."

But Scarlet's mind was drifting. *What can I get for five bones?* she wondered. *Maybe a broach? A bracelet? A...boa?*

"And Darling," said Daisy, putting her hands on her daughter's shoulders. "Try to focus. Remember what your father said."

"Forewarned is forearmed," said Dr. Sigmund.

"Oh, and Scarlet," said Daisy. "Keep an eye out for your nose."

"It's easier than keeping a nose out for your eye," said Dr. Sigmund, smiling.

It was true. Zombie body parts sometimes got separated from their owners, but they had an innate homing instinct. It was quite common to be out in a field or in some back alley of Plainfield or in the forest and see a hand or a foot crawling toward home.

Scarlet thought of her own nose, lost long ago on a first-grade field trip in the forest. She imagined it lying sad and alone, trying to move itself with little nostril flarings but not getting very far. Or worse, slowly digesting in the belly of a wild animal.

Her parents kept wanting to take her to Pick-A-Part to get a new nose. But Scarlet held out. She wanted to give the nose a little more time to find her. She wanted to feel whole from her own parts, not someone else's hand-me-down.

"One more thing," said Dr. Sigmund. He took off his watch and handed it to her. "So you can keep track of time."

Daisy forced a jar into Scarlet's other hand. The wet and writhing mass inside was partially obscured by the label, which read: Prime Time Snackin' Slugs. "For the protein," said Daisy.

Scarlet strapped on the watch and stuck the jar of slugs in her shoulder bag along with the cloak. Something shifted a little inside her. Just for a moment, she imagined she was outside her body. She saw herself through Daisy and Dr. Sigmund's eyes, feeling how they would feel saying goodbye to her. She felt a surge of love for her parents and clasped them both in a hug. "Thanks, Mom and Dad."

They squeezed her back.

"Don't muss your hair, now," said Daisy gently.

"Do you feel ready?" asked Dr. Sigmund.

She looked up at them and shook her head. "Not really."

Dr. Sigmund squeezed her shoulder. "That's normal," he said.

"Growing up isn't a bad thing," said Daisy.

"In fact," Dr. Sigmund winked at her, "it should be an adventure."

"But, yes, it *is* a bit scary sometimes," finished Daisy.

Scarlet nodded, swallowing the lump in her throat. "See you tonight," she said. And with that, she was out the door.

Dr. Sigmund closed the door softly behind her. He and Daisy looked at each other. Neither one spoke for a few moments. Dr. Sigmund unsnapped his jawbone. The *CLACK-click* sounded loud in the empty house.

He stared at his wrist. It looked lonely without the watch.

Daisy's hands fluttered about, seeking something to tidy.

Chapter Five
Zombies Roam the Street

M arket day!
    Plainfield Avenue teemed with zombies.
  Zombies teetering and tottering, wobbling and weaving, schlepping and shuffling down the cobbled, mobbed, and mudpuddled promenade.

At their feet crawled stray parts trying to find their way home. The fingers patiently pulling arms forward. Heels digging in and inching legs onward. Ears and noses advancing in tiny flexings.

Scarlet joined the throng.

She waved to a pair of grownups lurching past, "Hi, Mrs. and Mr. Festerson," she said to a couple walking by and came down the steps.

"Oh, hello Scarlet," said Mungo Festerson. Scarlet, as always, was attuned to what everyone was wearing. Jeminy had come up with the Threadheads motto—"clothes make the zombie"—and they were words Scarlet lived by. And judged by. As Mr. Festerson spoke, she saw that his suit was worn thin at the elbows and knees. "Hey," he said, "you should bring your folks by the cafe. We've got a new special, country-fried brainsteaks."

"With an insect-reduction sauce," smiled his wife, Swillda, who, Scarlet noticed, had a rip in her dress. "It's always different."

"Depends on the bugs we find in the morning," Mungo beamed.

The Festersons lurched on.

Mr. and Mrs. Sputum gimped up in dirt-stained dungarees and matching flannel work shirts rolled to the elbows. They flitted about, trying to contain the tumbling chaos of their shoddily clad boys—Roscoe, Loogie, Wocka-Wocka, Jethro, Pee-Wit, and Astro. The boys together were more like one mega-boy, a whirling mass of arms and legs noogie-ing each other's hair and tripping each other and playing keep-away with an ear they'd found.

Except Astro, a boy from her class. He was walking apart from his brothers, immersed in a book. Scarlet fell in alongside him. "Hi, Astro. Whatcha reading?"

"Huh?" Astro looked up from his book. "Oh, h-hi Scarlet." He blushed. "It's called Night of the Living Living. It's really scary. It's about…"

"She doesn't care, Brainless," said Roscoe. Astro only had a moment to wave at Scarlet before he was yanked into the brotherly melee.

Scarlet fell in behind the Gallowses, Hallowses, and Oozes, all decked out fine suits and dresses, shambling in an orderly line with their children clustered behind them.

"Morning," said Scarlet to Sparkle and Spangle Gallows.

Scarlet didn't expect a reply. She didn't get one. The twins didn't talk to Scarlet much in class or in the Threadheads, unless it was to mock her fashion sense. So it didn't surprise her that their only response now was to give her a glance-and-sneer.

Scarlet couldn't help but stare closely at their capes, their boas, their hats. She tried, but failed to find anything wrong with what they were wearing. *That's okay*, she thought, *wait 'til I get my dreams cape*.

Mrs. Ooze was lurching along on another new pair of designer legs. Scarlet examined the legs closely, and giggled when she realized that the left one was longer than the right.

Scarlet heard a booming voice behind her and turned to see Squire Cerebellum Augustus Stubbs bustling around and past the slower-moving zombies. "Excuse me, pardon me," he kept muttering over-loudly, consulting, as always, his giant neckwatch.

Scarlet checked the time on her father's watch, hanging loosely from her wrist. 11:30. Time already seemed to be zooming past.

She hurried on.

Scarlet passed the last of the mold-dappled brownstones of the Festerings, Plainfield's most fashionable neighborhood (according to Daisy, anyway).

She inhaled the sweet smell of rancid rubbish a-skitter with rat packs and glistening with tribes of slugs.

Despite her feeling anxious about Project Haggis and the rot mitzvah and growing up in general, Scarlet also felt something new—an exhilarating sense of freedom.

She pulled a slug from her snack jar and slurped it down.

Market Day!

Chapter Six
A Friend Who Looks Like an Enemy

The crowds squeezed in all around Scarlet as she neared the market. "Hey, careful," she said to the small of a back. "Ow! Watch it!" she told an elbow. "Mmpf. Careful…whoops!" Something tripped Scarlet and she fell, which caused her to do four things: gash her knee, tear her dress, rip her jacket, and spatter herself with mud.

She looked around at the parade of legs passing all around her. "Who tripped me?"

Something pinched her calf. A stray arm.

Scarlet grabbed it. "Bad arm! Bad!"

The arm poked her face. Scarlet leaned back. "Easy there, Pokey." The arm flexed and flailed, but Scarlet gripped it tight.

She was puzzling how to get herself to her feet when she felt two hands grip her shoulders from behind, lift her to her feet, and set her by the sidewalk, still holding Pokey the Arm.

She turned her head, but all she could see was the back of a man-zombie in a blue-checked workshirt disappearing into the crowd.

What an ugly shirt, she thought.

Scarlet felt a pinch at her side. "Stop it, Pokey!" The arm went limp and started to shake.

"Oh," said Scarlet. "You're scared." She held Pokey to her face and whispered to its hand. "Poor thing. It's going to be okay."

Sensing its moment, the hand smacked her cheek.

"You little…" Scarlet was so angry she wasn't sure how to finish the sentence. "I should just leave you here."

The hand circled its index finger.

"Fine," said Scarlet. She tossed Pokey onto an especially rancid rubbish heap and walked away. When she glanced back, she couldn't help thinking Pokey looked a little lonely.

Scarlet took a quick self-inventory. Torn jacket. Gashed knee. Mud-splatted dress. Hair beginning to wilt. For a moment, she thought about heading home to rearrange herself, but thoughts of the dreams cape kept her going. Besides, the market was just across the street.

Long ago, the Plainfield Sanitary Market had started as a lonely country store. But as the town of Plainfield grew up, so did the market, making up its architecture as it went along until it became a maze of shops and stalls where both Plainfielders and out-of-town zombies gathered every Saturday.

Scarlet entered the market and beelined it to the Mighty Offal, Mr. Chunk Grissom's gut shop.

A signboard helpfully showed what offal was (animal innards) and what his specialty haggis was (innards stuffed in a stomach). You could buy the haggis prepared whole or you could buy it by the piece ("some assembly required").

Chunk was a short zombie who wore faded yellow overalls and stood atop an overturned crate handing out the haggi as fast as he and his son, Chunk Jr., could wrap them up. Chunk Jr. was a classmate of Scarlet's. All she knew about him was that he loved helping his dad sell haggi and he liked to explore the woods outside Plainfield. Scarlet noticed he was dressed in faded yellow overalls like his father, only his had been patched and sealed many times.

Chunk Jr.'s face lit up. He waved at Scarlet.

She gave a condescending nod and turned to watch Chunk Sr. serenade his customers with the Mighty Offal jingle.

"*My offal's awful...delicious that is.*
Everyone knows...how nutritious it is.
But they don't know...how auspicious it is.
This is what offal...all wishes it is."

It was only when Scarlet rounded a corner that she saw how long the line was. Her face fell. If she had been her dad, her jaw might have fallen to the ground. The line went on and on, all the way to the back of the market.

Scarlet was distracted by a hubbub near the front of the line. A grownup zombie named Tom Femur took a staggering step backward after he was shoved by the girl in front of him.

"Stop squishing me!" the girl yelled.

Scarlet's spirits rose. It was a girl from her class. The weird one who always wore those horrible homemade clothes. What was her name? Scarlet couldn't remember. She had a nickname. Something "Bear."

"Hey," Scarlet called, shuffling toward her. "Hey, Bear…Girl?"

Bear Girl. That was it.

The girl gave a toss of her slimy hair and squinted at Scarlet, slowly chewing a massive wad of bubble cud.

"Hi, uh, Bear Girl," Scarlet said with forced cheer. "How's it going?" Scarlet ignored the frowns of the zombies in the line. The girl was wearing a pair of cutoff jeans and a faded sweatshirt with a crudely painted bear paw on it. As if the paw print wasn't enough, the girl also wore a carved wooden bear totem on a cord around her neck. Scarlet noticed that she was barefoot, and that her feet were different sizes. The left foot was size six, Scarlet guessed. The right looked like a size nine. *Total hand-me-down,* thought Scarlet.

"Are your feet..."

"Yeah," said the girl. She blew a massive bubble and let it pop. "So?"

Scarlet glanced at the scowling grownups around her. "Nothing. They're...nice." She moved closer and said in a low voice, "Listen, Bear Girl. Can you do me a favor?"

The girl held out a palm. "'Bear Girl?'"

"Um, yeah. I thought you were called that." Scarlet shifted nervously.

"I hate that name. That's what your fash 'n' bash friends call me."

"Oh, they're not my friends..." Scarlet paused. Weren't they? No, not really. But she also didn't want to be lectured to by a...a bear freak in a homemade T-shirt. "They...I mean we...we're called the Threadheads."

Pop went the bubble cud.

The line moved forward a few steps.

Scarlet stared at the girl, as if seeing her for the first time. "What DO you want to be called?"

"My name."

"What's your name?" asked Scarlet.

"LaMort. Moldylocks LaMort." *Pop.*

Scarlet looked at her dad's watch, starting to worry, just a little bit, about the time. "Okay. Moldylocks. Will you give me cuts?"

Moldylocks stared at Scarlet. "No."

Scarlet had an inspiration. "You like slugs?" She reached into her shoulder bag and pulled out the snackin' slugs. She held the jar out to Moldylocks.

Moldylocks took the jar, unscrewed the lid and guzzled a mouthful.

Scarlet went to step in front of Moldylocks, but Moldylocks stopped her and jerked her thumb behind her. "Backsies," she said through a mouthful of slugs.

"Deal," Scarlet nodded.

Scarlet stepped in front of Tom Femur, who immediately turned to the zombie behind him and said, "Save my place."

Before Scarlet's smile had faded, she felt two massive hands grip her under the arms and carry her along—past Tso Delicious, past Beyond Be-Leaf, past Phartball's Phabrics—past stall after stall after stall until they reached the back of the line. Tom Femur set her down. "You seem like a nice girl," he said. "But the Mighty Offal is a backsies-free zone." He was laughing as he walked away.

This was the moment when Scarlet could have prevented all the trouble that came later. She could have stayed at the back of the line, flowing slowly toward the haggis counter listening to Chunk Grissom Sr. sing his offal songs, playing out dreams of capes in her noseless head.

She could have and she may have, if Jeminy Stinkpit hadn't at that moment come walking by.

Everyone has a Jeminy Stinkpit. That one zombie who seems to have been unearthed for the singular purpose of making your undeath as miserable as possible. The one who pushes your buttons—the buttons labeled "You're not smart" and "You're not talented" and "You're not fashionable" and "You're not enough."

Jeminy, who never seemed to go anywhere without a posse, was Scarlet's number-one button-pusher. And today she was flanked by LuAnn Fumarole and Sparkle and Spangle Gallows.

Scarlet edged behind the portly zombie in front of her, hoping the girls hadn't seen her.

They had.

A smile twisted across Jeminy's face. "Ooh, look girls. Fashion emergency, aisle nine." The gaggle of girls giggled as they passed her by.

Drive-by ridicule. Apparently Scarlet wasn't even worth stopping to make fun of. And to make the shame worse, all four of them looked fabulous.

"Forget this!" she growled and stomped out of line.

She didn't know where she was going. She just let her feet take her while she cursed everything she could think of to curse. Jeminy. Her parents. Moldylocks. Long lines. Haggis. Pokey the Arm.

Growing up. She even cursed her Grandma, then immediately felt terrible, and uncursed her.

Scarlet finally got around to cursing herself.

After a while, when she was worn out with cursing, she felt the market start to work its magic on her.

Her senses were beset.

The smell of leather and lacquer from the craft stalls. The *clinka-binka* and *clanga-banga* of the jewelsmiths snipping silver and hammering brass. The harangue of shopkeepers and artisans shouting "best deals" or "one of a kind" or "fresh 'n' tasty moldin' oldies." Buskers and bug mongers. Acrobats and artifacts. Shouts from the limb-menders and brainbakers and bedmat vendors and broom makers. Clouds of cleaning-solvent stenches mixed with the aroma of zombie perfumes. And wafting through it all, the smells of fetid fungi, tainted tubers, spoiled sardines, rancid rump steaks, and ripe tripe.

Scarlet lost track of time.

She wandered dreamlike through the heart of the day. She listened, watched, tested perfumes, tasted samples, applauded performances, and she inhaled everywhere the musky mist of brains. Brains pickled and poached; blackened and barbecued; pan-fried, deep-fried, and stir-fried; canned and candied; caramelized and tenderized; dipped and whipped; pan-seared and mustard-smeared; marinated, disintegrated; boiled, broiled, and oiled; breaded and braised; baked and basted; grilled and chilled; honey-glazed and mayonaissed; decayed, sautéed, home-made. And raw.

When she came to herself, it was deep in the afternoon and she was standing in front of the dreams cape.

Chapter Seven
An Enemy Who Looks Like a Friend

The dreams cape took pride of place at the front of the Elysian fashion stall, adorning a zombie-quin mounted atop a pedestal ringed with tea candles.

Scarlet shambled closer, forgetting to breathe.

The cape was like a clear night sky made of fabric, star-filled and shimmery, billowing gently on the faint drafts swirling through the market, whispering to Scarlet of things grown up and graceful.

But when she bent to peer at the price tag, she felt as though she would decompose on the spot. "A hundred bones," she moaned. She opened her coin purse and counted out the coins. She had twenty, the five her parents had given her plus fifteen for the haggis.

"It's just your size," purred a voice over her shoulder. Scarlet turned, looking into the face of the impossibly elegant shopkeeper.

Dame Lurk approached her, the picture of undead refinement. Tall and thin, she didn't so much lurch as glide, and as she did, her evening gown rippled softly in her wake. She placed one immaculately buffed arm over Scarlet's shoulders and drew a picture in the air with her free hand.

"I can see you now. The girl with grace. The jewel of school. The belle of the ball. Yes," the shopkeeper cooed, "you were unearthed for this cape."

"But it's a hundred," said Scarlet. "And I only have twenty."

Dame Lurk removed her arm from Scarlet's shoulder. She smiled sympathetically and clasped her hands. "It is a pity, but perhaps," Dame Lurk nodded at Scarlet's bag, "you have something to sell?"

Scarlet slapped her forehead. "Of course!" She opened her bag and held it out so Dame Lurk could see the cloak. "It's really…durable," Scarlet explained.

"Indeed," said Dame Lurk, frowning. Her tone became businesslike. "Pawn shop. Back of the market."

Scarlet nodded and scuttled off, completely forgetting her parents' warning about the strange strangers at the back of the market.

As she waited in the pawn-shop line, she calculated how much she could get for the cloak. Maybe she'd get more money if she described it not as "old," but "vintage." And maybe she'd be able to get a few bones for the shoulder bag, too. "Bargain with confidence," Scarlet had told herself.

In the end, Scarlet couldn't do it.

She couldn't let her Grandmother down.

So Scarlet wandered, lost in swirling thoughts, until her sequin-sneakered feet took her to the shop that would change her undeath: "Barnaby B's Boas. Imported Organic Necksessories."

The stall was narrow and gloriously overstuffed with feather boas of every bird imaginable. And some UN-imaginable.

Scarlet scanned the labels. There were feathers from birds she knew, like crows and vultures, some from birds she'd heard of, like egrets and eidolons, and some from birds thought to be extinct, like archaeopteryxes and quintilidons.

It wasn't just the feathers, though, it was the craft that had gone into making them. The feathers were woven together so tightly it seemed there still might be a bird underneath them. A formal-dress boa constructed of peacock feathers. A foul-weather boa of duck feathers. Bower bird boas bedecked in charms and trinkets. Pigeon-feather boas to wear when exercising.

If she couldn't buy the dreams cape, maybe Scarlet could afford a boa. *After all, it IS my unearthday.* She trailed her fingers along the boas spilling out of the sale rack at the front of the stall.

"Now here's a neck in need of feathering if ever I saw one," said a buttery smooth voice. Scarlet turned and beheld the shopkeeper, tall and sinewy. Dark eyes, a massive nose, a tidy goatee. His head was wrapped in a paisley silk scarf studded with bright gems. He strode toward Scarlet, his peacock-feather boa fluttering as he moved. He was captivating. He was disorienting.

"Well, now. Aren't you the *rara avis*," he purred.

"The what?" Scarlet stammered.

"The rare bird. The rarest of all, in fact: a woman *a la mode*."

Scarlet smiled, blushing. "A woman?"

"Of fashion," said the shopkeeper.

"Well…I guess I am today," said Scarlet. "It's my 13th unearthday."

The shopkeeper bowed. "*Felicitations in excelsis.*"

"What?" She thought his words were as glittery as his boas.

"Congratulations to the utmost. 13th, hmm? Now that is no common thing. Why, you've become a grownup."

"Nobody else seems to be noticing," said Scarlet, glowing.

"Most zombies don't see anything but themselves." The shopkeeper paused. "How rude of me. Introductions." He bowed once more. "Behold, before you stands Barnaby B. Wolf. My feet are fashionably booted. My suit is perfectly suited. Fashion's my modus operandi. Note the bowler, the vest. The many ruffles on my chest." He gestured with gloved hands as he spoke. "I twirl my cane in the air and I move without care."

Scarlet grinned. Barnaby B. Wolf grinned back.

What big teeth he had.

"So, my dear…"

"…Scarlet."

"So, my dear Scarlet. I daresay a boa would complement your satin jacket perfectly." His eyes flicked, down-up. "Tear or no."

His eyes were kind.

What big eyes he had.

"Actually, there's more. Worse-more."

"Oh? Do tell."

"My parents want me to wear…" Scarlet opened

her bag and pulled out a corner of the nasty cloak. "…this. It's a hand-me-down."

Barnaby wrinkled his nose, aghast.

What a big nose he had.

Barnaby whispered across the back of his hand. "Just between us, I wouldn't be caught undead in that thing."

"I know!" Scarlet zipped the bag closed. "Some unearthday, huh?"

"Well, maybe we can make it a bit better, starting now." Barnaby steered Scarlet to a rack of medium-priced boas.

"I don't know," said Scarlet. "I mean they're beautiful, but I don't think I can afford them."

"What's your budget, Darling?"

"I have to buy a haggis," said Scarlet. "That's another thing! Why am I doing chores on my unearthday?"

"The injustice flabbergasts me," he agreed.

"I only have five extra bones."

"Well, I think we can make that work. Why don't you take your pick. Any boa in the store. Yours for five."

Scarlet was stunned. "Really?" She rushed to hug Barnaby and on an impulse she said, "Would you like to come to my unearthday party?"

"I wouldn't dream of missing it," he said, licking his lips. "I do so love zombies."

"What?" asked Scarlet.

"I love the..." Barnaby paused, "...the company of zombies. Just tell me where the festivities are taking place and I shall be there."

She gave Barnaby her grandmother's address and in moments she'd chosen a cardinal-and-swan-feather boa. Red and white in equal measure.

As she left the shop, she flung the boa over her shoulder with a flourish. So fashionable. So grown-up. She walked to the front of the market, hoping Jeminy and the Threadheads would see her now.

If she had looked back, she would have noticed that Barnaby was closing up shop early.

CHAPTER EIGHT
TIME TO DO THE RIGHT THING

There were only a few zombies waiting at the Mighty Offal. Still, Scarlet made a show of walking slowly to the end of the line, twirling her boa.

Chunk Grissom Sr. moved gracefully behind the counter, beginning to close up the shop.

And he sang, softer than he had in the morning.

I've got guts and I've got stuff
Stop your shopping, I'm enough
Always tender never tough
Get yourself up off your duff
I won't give you any guff
You'll love my guts and other stuff!"

When Scarlet reached the counter, Chunk Jr.'s tired face lit up.

"Hi, Scarlet. That's some necklace!"

"Necklace?" she snorted. "It's a custom imported feather boa."

Chunk Jr. gave an embarrassed laugh. "Oh, right. A boa! I knew that. I LOVE snakes."

Scarlet rolled her eyes. "Can I just get a haggis?" Scarlet asked, caressing the boa and looking around to see if anyone noticed her.

Chunk Jr. swallowed and nodded. He cleared his throat and said softly, "I saw you earlier. I saved you our best one. That wasn't really nice of Mr. Femur."

Scarlet looked up from her boa. "Hmm?"

"Right," said Chunk Jr. He retrieved a massive haggis from under the counter. "Our signature offering," he said. He wrapped the haggis in just the right amount of wax paper, bound it neatly with twine, and presented it to Scarlet. "Voila! The mondo-haggis."

"Nice," said Scarlet distractedly.

She paid him and placed the mondo-haggis in her bag. Before she could go, Chunk Jr. pulled a small package out of his pocket and set it on the counter. It was wrapped and bound, much as the haggis was.

"I'm good," said Scarlet, turning.

"It's a present," he said gently. "Happy unearthday."

"Oh, thank you," stammered Scarlet, surprised. "How did you know?"

"I heard you talking in class."

Scarlet untied the knot. "Is it a broach? A pendant? I love accessories."

"Uh…it's sort of an accessory," Chunk Jr. stammered.

Scarlet ripped open the paper and froze. She looked at the gift. Looked at Chunk Jr. "Not even close." She whirled away, leaving the package on the counter.

When she exited the market, she was shocked to discover it was almost dark outside. She looked at her father's watch. Four o'clock? How'd it get to be four?! The streets were almost empty—just a few zombies lurching home. Even the stray limbs seemed to have wandered off or found shelter for the night.

Scarlet wrapped the boa tight around her neck. It wasn't as soft as she thought it would be. Or as warm. "I'm supposed to be at Grandma's in an hour," she muttered. "It's going to be a cold walk."

"You still have time," said a voice behind her.

Scarlet looked behind her. A wiry older zombie leaning on a broom stared at her thoughtfully. He wore patched overalls and a long-sleeved blue-checked workshirt.

"Time for what?" she asked.

"Time to do the right thing."

Scarlet noticed something wiggling. "You have something in your chest pocket," she said.

The man laughed and pulled out an unattached hand. "That's Carlito. He's my helping hand. He showed up at my doorstep one evening—guess he was looking for the previous owner—and I didn't have the heart to turn him away." He stepped toward Scarlet and held out his hand, the one attached to his right arm. "I'm Carl. I keep the market clean."

Scarlet shook Carl's attached hand. She remembered her parents' warning about strange strangers, but she had a good feeling about Carl.

"Everyone needs a helping hand sometimes, don't you think?"

Scarlet nodded. "I guess so...What do you mean 'time to do the right thing?'"

Carl set Carlito back in his shirt pocket. "That's for you to decide."

Those sleeves, thought Scarlet. "You helped me today. You picked me up! How can I thank you?"

"Just pass it on," said the custodian. "Now, if you'll excuse me."

He resumed his sweeping.

Scarlet rushed back into the market.

Chunk Jr. was wiping the last of the haggis crumbs off the counter while his father stacked empty display crates. He saw Scarlet, but said nothing.

"Chunk Jr.….I…I'm sorry," said Scarlet. "Do you still have it? The present."

He nodded once.

"I didn't even try it on. Can I? It might fit."

He pulled the package out of his pocket and handed it to her.

It was a nose. An old woman's nose. Veined, warty, bulbous.

She wedged it in her nosehole and struck a pose. "Am I glamorous or what?"

Chunk Jr. burst out laughing. "I don't know WHAT I was thinking."

Scarlet laughed with him. "You were thinking of me. Thank you." She removed the nose. "Are you doing anything later? Want to come to my party?"

No, and yes.

"Okay. My Grandma's. Six o'clock. You know where she lives?"

He did.

"By the way," Scarlet added, "it's casual so you don't need to change. Overalls are perfect."

She regarded the nose, trembling in the palm of her hand. "Don't worry, Sniffy, I'll find a home for you." She paused. "And maybe a friend." She tucked the nose in her bag, waved goodbye to Chunk, and hustled out of the market.

Scarlet sped across the street with the-now heavy shoulder bag banging against her side. When she got to the refuse pile where she'd left Pokey, she stopped, looking all around her.

He hadn't gone far. She found him inching up a rain spout, pried him loose, and tucked him safely in her bag.

Scarlet headed into the dark.

Chapter Nine
Night Descends on Scarlet

Scarlet kicked at blown-down branches as she trundled along the dimming streets. Plainfield's streetlamps were coughing awake but their lights were feeble flickers against the dusk. She adjusted her shoulder bag, tucked her torn jacket tight around her, and snugged the boa around her neck.

Scarlet entered the forest. She shivered, not so much from the cold as from the itchy feeling of the unfamiliar and the sounds of rustlings and danger all around.

The *rat-a-tat-a-tat* of a deadpecker. *Kero-keroak* from a cluster of crickets. *Whaddup-whaddup-whaddup* of the slimytoads. A meadow of Venus flytraps, their tiny mouths snapping shut on their wriggling insect meals—*click-click-click*.

Scarlet shuddered, but trudged on. Night descended completely and the path through the woods became a tunnel. A twig snapped and something heavy slithered wetly in the undergrowth. Off in the direction of Grandma's house, a wolf howled.

She looked at her dad's watch, but couldn't tell the time in this utter dark. *Why was I so distracted? I could have been at Grandma's by now.*

The bag wriggled.

"You okay in there Pokey? Sniffy?" she said aloud.

The wriggling continued.

Scarlet thought of her friends and their families. In a little while, they'd be clomping cheerfully along this same path, swinging lanterns and singing back the darkness.

"Hey, you guys want a song?" she asked the bag. She didn't wait for an answer.

"*The woods are undead,*" she quavered, "*with the sound of mucus.*"

A raven squawked from a pinetop.

"*With zombies they chew,*" she sang a little louder, "*for a thousand years...*"

A bolt of lightning lit the forest. Scarlet saw a hundred pairs of eyes gleaming back at her. Then they were gone.

"*They in-fest my brain,*" she whispered, "*with the sound of mucus.*"

A low roll of thunder drummed down. The sound made her cower.

"*My gut wants to spew...each song...it hears.*"

The sky burst open. Rain began to pummel Scarlet. Her hair soon gave up all aspirations of style and sagged to her skull, her satin jacket soaked through, and her boa wilted.

Scarlet shook a fist at the sky. "Okay, fine! You win!" She set her shoulder bag down in the mud and fished out the old cloak. Pokey clung to the sleeve. Scarlet pulled him off, which made him angry. He reached for her, grabbing at anything he could get a grip on until she managed to shove him back into the bag and zip it shut. Mostly shut.

His middle finger was caught in the zipper.

"Oh, sorry!" said Scarlet.

She pushed the finger back in and closed the bag.

Scarlet wrapped the cloak around her and pulled up the hood.

Warmer now, she considered the world from Pokey's perspective. He was alone, scared, and had no idea where he was going.

Scarlet opened the bag and reached for Pokey. She held his hand 'til he relaxed, then took Sniffy and placed her in Pokey's palm. Sniffy's nostrils flared in-out-in-out, then slowed as Pokey's fingers cradled her.

"Hang on, friends," cooed Scarlet. "We'll be at Grandma's soon."

Scarlet zippered the bag and slung it back over her shoulder. Now armored against the night in her cloak, Scarlet didn't feel quite so afraid. The thorny branches scratched harmlessly at the cloak's tough exterior. Raindrops hit the cloak and beaded to the ground. The wind howled because it couldn't find a way in.

Scarlet passed Kobayashi Rockpile and the cutoff to O'Putrid's Pond. She was getting close.

*I wonder what presents people got me. The dreams cape! Jeminy is going to be so jealous...*Scarlet suddenly felt tired of thinking about Jeminy. To her surprise, she also felt tired of thinking about the dreams cape.

The path rose as she trudged toward the Uplands and crossed Mollie Tinkle Creek. Almost there. She rounded a familiar cluster of gnarled pines that hung heavily with scarves of moss and there it was—Grandma's house. But it was barely visible.

Scarlet had expected to see light spilling out into the yard, but the house was almost completely dark. There was only the faint flicker of a single candle from the downstairs hall.

The girl in her thought, *Well, THIS is just leechy. I wonder if she even remembered my unearthday.* But as Scarlet shambled to the front door, the grownup in her thought something was amiss. Her skin began to crawl, and it wasn't from skinbugs.

Knock. Knock. Knock. "Grandma?...Grandma? It's me, Scarlet."

She peeked through the window beside the front door and saw a figure striding up the front hall. The thing was Grandma-shaped, but...not. It was taller than Grandma. It moved with unnatural grace. Still, even in the dim light, Scarlet recognized Grandma's beret and her billowy muumuu, cinched as always, with a macramé belt.

The door flew open.

"Come in, come in, child. It's warm inside!" said the figure.

Scarlet stared at the collar of the muumuu. At the lone feather poking up from under the collar. A peacock feather.

She took a step back.

She stared into Grandma's face.

It wasn't Grandma's face.

"Barnaby?"

Scarlet didn't have time to scream. Barnaby swallowed her whole—cloak, boa, shoulder bag and all.

Down she slid.

Chapter Ten
All the Adventure Scarlet Can Stomach

Scarlet's whole undeath flashed before her eyes during that trip down Barnaby's gullet. Her world had always been full of dark and ordinary things, but it was only now, at the end, that she truly appreciated them.

How her bedroom leaked shadows. How Chucky Moldfish greeted her grumpily each morning. The way mold bloomed on walls. The scritch of a quill on paper. All Plainfield's clatter and quiet. Chunk Jr. and Moldylocks and friendships she might have had. And her mom and dad. They could be so annoying. And so kind. Scarlet grieved it all.

She landed with a squelch on the spongy floor of Barnaby's stomach. As she struggled to her knees, stomach juice splashed her feet. Scarlet felt herself sway. Barnaby must be moving through the house. For the moment, Scarlet was too curious to panic. She felt about her for something useful, guessing at the objects she touched. Watermelon rind…fish skeleton…squirrel…well, part of a squirrel…zombie?

Amid the sour stomach stench, Scarlet smelled something familiar.

Perfume.

Low Tide No. 5.

"Grandma?!"

"What the fungus!" said a voice in the wet dark. "Is that you, Braindrop?"

"You're still undead?"

"You betcha, Picklebutt! I just dozed off and didn't hear you come in. Happy unearthday!"

Scarlet hugged her Grandmother in the squishy dark.

"So how do you like being a grownup so far?" asked Grandma Bone.

"It's horrible! Chores, lines at the market, my jacket has a tear, my boa is a mess and…wait, what am I saying? What are we going to do?"

"I don't know, Scardy Girl. Whatcha got in mind?"

"Me? I thought you would have an idea!"

"Hmm. Let me think for a minute." Grandma Bone was silent for about two seconds. "I got it."

"Yes," Scarlet leaned in closer.

"Ow!" Scarlet felt a finger poke her chest. "I think Pokey got out."

"No, that's me," said Grandma Bone.

"What's your answer?"

"That's it. And who's Pokey?"

"Your answer to getting us out of here is to poke me? He's a stray. A friend, I mean."

"Ah. Maybe he can help. You gotta stop thinking with your head." Grandma Bone poked Scarlet's forehead. "And think from HERE." She poked Scarlet's chest again. "From the inside. From your undead center."

Scarlet was skeptical. "How?"

"Just let the answer happen," said Grandma Bone. "Is that the cloak I felt? I don't remember it having feathers."

"It's a feather boa I got today," said Scarlet.

"That's a nice touch. It's a good cloak, but it needed some modernizing."

"Well, it *was* a feather boa." Scarlet pictured herself and suddenly started to giggle. The cloak now smelled like wolf stomach. Her boa was a limp string of damp feathers. Her hair a sodden tangle. Her nosehole a snot factory. Her shoes shorn of sequins. She shook with laughter.

"What is it, Scarlet?" asked Grandma.

"I was just imagining what the Threadheads would think if they saw me," she gasped. "They'd hurl." Grandma Bone started to laugh and the two held each other, shaking at the absurdity of it all.

Suddenly Scarlet shouted, "Grandma! That's it!"

CHAPTER ELEVEN
WHAT GOES DOWN MUST COME UP

"What's it?" sputtered Grandma.

"We'll make him hurl!"

"Great idea, Scarly. Tickle his epiglottis!"

"His what?"

"The dangly thing in your throat. It always worked on your father when he was just learning to lurch. He'd always eat any little object he could get his hands on. Buttons, marbles, thumbtacks. I don't know how many times I'd have to induce puking. Never from the inside, of course. Still, worth a try."

Scarlet found her balance and reached her arm up Barnaby's throat. All she could feel was gullet stretching upward. How did I ever squeeze through that? she wondered. She pulled her arm back down. "I can't reach."

"Funny how your father grew up to be so cautious now," said Grandma. "Always warning people about this and that."

"Grandma! Help me think!" urged Scarlet. "Wait, what?"

"He's so cautious. You know how he's always saying 'forewarned…'"

"…is forearmed!' Pokey!" Scarlet reached into her shoulder bag and hugged the arm to her chest. "I need you, my friend." She slowly unclenched his fingers and removed Sniffy. Pokey convulsed. Scarlet held him close. When he'd calmed down, Scarlet whispered, "Make him hurl. You can do it." She stretched Pokey, fingers up high into Barnaby's throat.

Scarlet heard Barnaby cough, but that was all.

"It's not working!" moaned Scarlet.

"What does your undead center say?" urged Grandma.

"I don't know," moaned Scarlet. She pulled Pokey back down and set him in her lap. She put her hand inside her cloak, over her heart, over her boa.

Her boa.

She pulled off a feather and stuck the feather in Pokey's hand. He dropped it. She tried again and again he dropped it. And a third time.

"He's so stubborn!" Scarlet sobbed.

"He probably just doesn't know the feather," said Grandma Bone, wrapping an arm around Scarlet. "Got anything else in your bag of tricks?"

"I don't know. I don't know. I don't know."

"Well, you're just full of 'I don't knows,' aren't you?"

"I don't knows. I don't…nose."

Sniffy!

"Grandma, get ready. I'm going to take this feather and stick it in Sniffy's nostril."

"Which one?"

"Sniffy's the nose."

"I mean, which nostril?"

"I don't know. Does it matter?"

"I doubt it."

"Fine, the left nostril. I'm going to get on your shoulders. I'll give Sniffy to Pokey to hold. He'll protect her. I'll reach him up again so he can tickle Barnaby's dangly thing and puke us out. Arm. Nose. Feather. Hold tight. Got it?"

"Got it!"

Scarlet climbed on Grandma's shoulders and stretched as high as she could.

Barnaby felt a tickling in his throat. He felt a burning in his gullet. He felt a clenching in his belly. He wiggled and squirmed. Suddenly, he knew what was coming but was powerless to stop it.

Barnaby blinked.

Barnaby burped.

Barnaby barfed.

Chapter Twelve
TOTALLY GROSSOME

Out gushed Scarlet and Grandma Bone in a wash of wolf goo. Scarlet scrambled to her feet, rushed at Barnaby, and kicked him in the wolfnuts.

Grandma tackled Barnaby. *WHOOMF*. While Barnaby simultaneously howled in pain and gasped for air, Scarlet retrieved her boa from a puddle of wolf-bile and, after allowing herself a moment of regret for ruining such a beautiful fashion accessory, tied his forepaws behind him.

Together Grandma Bone and Scarlet wrestled Barnaby to the open front door. The wind blew in the rain. The zombies tossed out the wolf. Barnaby tumbled off the porch and landed *PLOP* in the mud of the yard.

Right at the feet of Daisy and Sigmund Bone, and a crowd of zombies behind them.

Scarlet gave a triumphant shout when she saw them—the Chunk Grissoms (junior and senior), Squire Cerebellum Augustus Stubbs (and his boys), schoolmates like Moldylocks, Hansel and Gretel Rictus, and Jack Rot. Scarlet was even almost happy to see a smirking Jeminy Stinkpit, flanked by Sparkle and Spangle Gallows. Scarlet sighed. Jeminy DID look amazing in her all-weather cloak and duck-feather boa.

Moldylocks grinned down at Barnaby. "That is totally grossome."

Jeminy, however, couldn't help being Jeminy. "Hey, Scarlet," she sneered. "Is that a cloak you're wearing? Or a carcass?"

Jeminy never saw the missile that hit her a moment later.

It was a missile in the shape of Moldylocks LaMort and it scored a direct hit.

Down went the girls and a writhing muddy tussle commenced. Moldylocks pinned Jeminy momentarily, unleashing a string of indecipherable curses and flailing her arms at Jeminy's head. Jeminy was bigger, though, and she recovered fast. Soon, she scored a reversal and held Moldylocks helpless beneath her. This was too much for Scarlet, who swooped in, shouldered Jeminy aside and lifted Moldylocks out of the mud.

By this time, the other grownups intervened to keep the two separate.

Thunder rumbled. Rain fell harder. Everyone was soaked.

"Hey, everybody," yelled Scarlet, "are we going to have a party or we gonna stay outside and let our skin rot?"

The zombies laughed. They started to move to the front door.

"Mom, Dad..." said Scarlet. "Can you grab Barnaby?"

Daisy and Dr. Sigmund looked about them.

Barnaby was gone.

CHAPTER THIRTEEN
WHAT DO YOU WISH FOR WHEN YOU HAVE EVERYTHING?

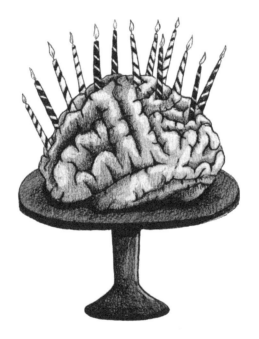

All that remained of Barnaby were two chewed-up boas and a trail of feathers quickly being blown into the night.

"I'll go!" yelled Chunk Sr. "Spasm, Retch, come with me. Everybody else go inside."

"I'll secure the perimeter!" shouted Dr. Sigmund.

Scarlet turned to Grandma Bone. "Did Dad really just say that?"

Grandma Bone laughed. "I'm sure we'll all feel safer knowing Plainfield's leading psychologist has 'secured the perimeter.'"

"Okay, boys," yelled Grandma to the men. "Go get him! Just be back in time for braincake!"

The zombies inside stripped off their soaked coats. Grandma built up the fire in the kitchen and Scarlet stoked the one in the front room. Together, they strung a clothesline in a zigzag through all the downstairs rooms.

Soon, coats and cloaks (and a feather boa or two) hung in steaming curtains. Zombies walked around in their long johns, union suits, T-shirts, and tighty-whiteys, chatting and laughing at themselves, and sipping hot mugs of Earl Gray Matter tea.

Grandma and Scarlet lurched into action, delivering trays of gut jerky, bowls of skin beetles, and containers of skin spackle for suppurating sores and scabbed skin.

The posse of wolf-hunters and perimeter-securers soon returned. Dr. Sigmund reported to the partygoers. "Folks, we tracked him as far as O'Putrid's Pond before the tracks disappeared. But don't worry—we've posted sentries..."

"'Posted sentries?'" Scarlet giggled to Grandma Bone.

"...at the front and back. Thanks to Carl and Tom for taking first watch. We should be safe. Later, we can all go home as a big group, but for now, let's have a party!"

The zombies cheered. Scarlet left to fetch a tray of sliced, raw mondo-haggis from the kitchen. When she re-entered the living room, she paused to look around. For the first time in her undeath, she felt like she was seeing zombies for who they were, not what they were wearing. And the zombies she saw were kind, surly, funny, boring, irascible, stubborn, joyous, and for the most part, a mix of all of those things and more.

The party kaleidoscoped into an array of colorful mini-conversations. Scarlet listened as she circulated with the haggis, while sentries rotated in and out every few minutes on wolf-watch.

Chunk Sr. talking to Phileas Batuta. "It was the strangest thing. The entire boa stall was just packed up and gone."

Moldylocks telling Jack, "You're full of mucus! Bears do exist."

Old Lady Poxball talking cooking with Chunk Jr. "Now, to get the best jerky, you gotta leave it in the smokehouse for a week." And Chunk Jr. replying, "Have you ever tried your jerky in a haggis?"

Tug Singlebuttock insisting to Kay Hamhock that he wasn't crazy. He really had seen lights in the sky. "It looked like a giant house. You gotta believe me."

Mr. Sever, Scarlet's science teacher, explaining to Constable Cruft: "I'm telling you, the kids have been bringing in some strange creatures from the woods. Snakes with feet. Possums with extra pairs of hands. Archie Dunphee even said he saw a rat the other day with two heads. It's not natural."

Daisy assuring Lyudmila Gallows that "property values are going to go up even more this year."

Anka Mastiff, the fortune-teller, asking Phylidia Phartball what she knew of circuses.

Dorothy J. LaMort, Moldylocks' mom, standing beside the piano, having a serious conversation with One Tuckerson and his younger brothers, Two and Three. "Have you boys done any musical theater? You'd be great in my next production."

Spasm Jenkins, Retch Lardbelly, and Carl Nugget leaning together in a corner speculating about the wolf's whereabouts.

And for the moment, the younger zombies had forgotten their tribes. They were all just undead kids laughing and telling stories. Jeminy caught Scarlet's eye and gave her a subtle nod.

Grandma Bone swept past and took the empty haggis tray from Scarlet.

A throat cleared behind her.

Moldylocks.

Scarlet beamed. "I didn't get a chance to thank you. You make a good missile."

Moldylocks shrugged. "I like a good scrap. Plus, I owed you."

"For what?"

Moldylocks reached into her pocket and handed Scarlet the jar of snackin' slugs. It was empty. She hugged Moldylocks. "Thanks for coming to my party," she whispered.

"Thanks for being my friend or whatever," muttered Moldylocks.

Just before Scarlet returned to the kitchen, she felt a hand on her shoulder.

"Nice going, Scarlet. You did the right thing today."

Scarlet looked at the hand. It was held by another hand.

Carl and Carlito! And Carl was wearing the same blue-checked work shirt he'd been wearing earlier.

Scarlet thanked him for his help at the market. "And by the way," she said. "I love your shirt."

The moment Scarlet returned to the kitchen, Grandma Bone looked up from a notepad she was scribbling in. "Go have fun. It's YOUR party, Braindrop."

"Just tell me how Pokey and Sniffy are doing!" laughed Scarlet.

Grandma Bone gestured to a straw-filled box set next to the stove. Sniffy was cuddled into Pokey's protective palm. Both were warm and sleeping soundly, despite the hubbub around them.

"Now, scoot!" said Grandma Bone.

Scarlet skedaddled back to the front room to relax at last.

A *tink-tink-tink* sound rang through the house as Dr. Sigmund tapped his jaw against his tea mug.

"Unnh. Nnnh." Dr. Sigmund put his jaw in. *Click-CLACK.* "Attention everyone, I'd like to sing Happy Unearthday to Scarlet—the most grown-up girl I know."

Daisy held a finger up, paused, and gave everyone the cue to begin singing. "And a one and a two..."

When the song was finished, Grandma Bone held a cake, bright with candles, before Scarlet.

"Make a wish."

Scarlet looked at the happy bedraggled zombies all around her and for a moment, didn't know what to wish for. She had everything she needed.

Moldylocks elbowed in front of Tom Femur, saying to him, "Stop squishing me!"

Scarlet looked at her bear-loving friend and she knew.

Chapter Fourteen
The Best Things Are Ings

No rot mitzvah was complete without gifts and music.

The townzombies crowded around Scarlet and plied her with presents—jars of bug jams, skull-embroidered scarves, tins of skin spackle, and one blue-checked handkerchief.

Daisy and Sigmund did indeed give Scarlet the dreams cape. And when she put it on, she felt like a beautiful night. She spun in place, letting the cape billow out around her, not caring any more who it would impress or make jealous. She just liked how it made her feel. Indeed, when she thought about it later, this was the moment she decided to resign from the Threadheads.

"We'd already put a down payment on the cape," Daisy explained. "There was no way Dame Lurk was going to be selling it to anyone today. Especially not you."

Scarlet was overwhelmed. "Thank you, Mom and Dad. Thank you everyone."

Her many friends filled the room with hoots and whoops.

"Now it's time for MY gift," said Grandma Bone.

"But you gave me the party," said Scarlet.

Grandma Bone cackled. "Nah. The best gifts are ings." She nodded toward the front of the great room, where Abercrombie, Winthrop, and Bash Stubbs had set up their musical instruments.

(When the Stubbs boys got together to play music, they became the Stubbz Boyz, Plainfield's awesomest party band.)

"I don't understand," said Scarlet.

"Well, the best times I've ever had have been when I've been do-ING something. Cook-ING, eat-ING, macrame-ING, surf-ING, and..." she held up one of her timeworn hands and gave the OK sign to the Stubbz Boyz, "rock-ING!"

At that moment, the twang of a guitar, a rhythmic pounding on the drums, and a voice as mellow as beach waves filled the room.

"This is for you, Scarlet," said Bash, "written special for you by Grandma Bone." He launched into song.

"Dreaming of new cloaks,
couldn't hear your folks,
telling you to just follow the rules.
You should have acted.
You got distracted,
looking at beads and at dreams capes and jewels."

"It's true!" laughed Scarlet, shaking her head.

The Boyz kicked into the chorus:

"Wastin' away down there inside of Barnaby.
Project Haggis was under assault.
Scarlet might claim
that others should be to blame
'Cause she knew...it was so not her fault."

The zombies of Plainfield got up and began to dance, ducking under the drying coats and dresses.

"Feeling at wit's end,
she found a new friend
with boas to help her accessorize.
She got the haggis,
entered the forest,
and forgot all about that strange gleam in his eyes."

"Don't talk to strange strangers, remember?" yelled Dr. Sigmund, whirling Daisy around the dance floor.

"Wastin' away down there inside of Barnaby.
Project Haggis was under assault.
She wanted to claim
that others were to blame
Then she thought...'Well, it could be my fault.'"

"Last verse, everyone," said Bash. "Repeat after me." He led them through, line by line.

"She found a new way,
Scarlet saved the day,
and learned that there's something she just hadn't seen.
You, too, can live large.
If you just take charge
without forgetting the things that you've been."

"Everybody now," sang Bash.

"Wastin' away down there inside of Barnaby.
Project Haggis was under assault.
Scarlet could claim
that maybe she was to blame,
and she's right. It so was her fault."

"Happy unearthday, Scarlet," said Bash.

The party went on and on into the night, with everyone eating and feasting and drinking and dancing and too many other INGs to mention.

Sometime in the wee small hours, the partygoers shambled back to Plainfield in one ragged cluster.

Scarlet wore her dreams cape beneath her cloak, her beautiful, warm, enduring, wolf-stomach-smelling cloak. The box containing Pokey and Sniffy was tucked safely under her arm.

She fell in alongside Moldylocks. "Want to know what I wished for?" asked Scarlet.

Moldylocks nodded.

"I couldn't think of anything for myself, so I made a wish for you."

"Really?"

"Yep. I wished you'd meet a bear."

Afterword
And May Your Morning Bring Rebirth

Scarlet made it most of the way home, but as they reached the edge of the Festerings neighborhood, the excitement of the day caught up with her and she started to stagger with fatigue.

Dr. Sigmund carried Scarlet the rest of the way home, up the steps to the Bone brownstone, and down to her cellar bedroom. Dr. Sigmund lay Scarlet in her dirtbox and tucked her cloak in around her. "I remember when this bed seemed too big for you," he whispered. "Time goes by so fast."

Daisy dropped a pinch of scumflakes into Chucky's tank, then shambled quietly to the row of dirtmasks hanging by Scarlet's bed. She ran her fingers slowly along each, finally settling on the one decorated with glowing worms and dancing spiders. It was the first dirtmask she and Dr. Sigmund had ever bought their daughter.

Daisy snugged the mask over Scarlet's mouth and nosehole, though it really was too small for her now. Cinching the drawstring behind her head, she whispered, "You always looked so peaceful in this one."

Dr. Sigmund thought of a nursery rhyme he and Daisy used to sing a long time ago. They sang it now.

"We'll scoop the dirt and dig the dirt.
You nestle snug into the earth.
May all your dreams be dark tonight.
And may your morning bring rebirth."

Chucky Moldfish simply said, "Blurp."

As they sang, Scarlet's thoughts drifted to something Moldylocks had said to her on the walk home. How Scarlet wasn't what Moldylocks thought she would be. How she was strong. Not like a "Scarlet." Like a "Scar."

Scar. She liked the sound of that.

She let the dirt cover her, happy to let her parents think she was dreaming.

Looking for your next great-read aloud book?

In this overbusy world, we make it easy for families to slow down and connect. Each week we send out our big-hearted, irreverent, smartly crafted stories—for free—the kind of stories you can't wait to read together.

Get a story in your inbox every week. Visit 320sycamorestudios.com or scan the QR code to find out more.

Happy reading!

320 Sycamore Studios

Made in the USA
Las Vegas, NV
28 January 2022